The
CARNIVAL
CAPER

AN INTERACTIVE MYSTERY ADVENTURE

by Steve Brezenoff
illustrated by Marcos Calo

Field Trip Mysteries Adventures
are published by Stone Arch Books
A Capstone Imprint
1710 Roe Crest Drive
North Mankato, Minnesota 55603
www.mycapstone.com

Library of Congress Cataloging-in-Publication Data is available online
Names: Brezenoff, Steven, author. | Calo, Marcos, illustrator. | Brezenoff,
Steven. Field trip mysteries.
Title: The carnival caper : an interactive mystery adventure / by Steve
Brezenoff ; illustrated by Marcos Calo.
Other titles: You choose books.
Description: North Mankato, Minnesota : Stone Arch Books, a Capstone
imprint, [2017] | Series: You choose stories. Field trip mysteries |
Summary: When the Franklin Middle School's sixth grade arrives at the
amusement park, they find that the electronic cards that serve as all
purpose tickets and game trackers have disappeared, so Sam, Egg, Gum,
and Cat set out to solve the mystery and save the class field trip—
and it is up to the reader to determine the course of their investigation.
Identifiers: LCCN 2016040634| ISBN 9781496526458 (library binding) | ISBN
9781496526533 (ebook (pdf)) | ISBN 9781496526496 (pbk.) | ISBN 9781496526533 (ebook pdf)
Subjects: LCSH: School field trips—Juvenile fiction. | Amusement parks—
Juvenile fiction. | Theft—Juvenile fiction. | Plot-your-own stories. |
Detective and mystery stories. | CYAC: Mystery and detective stories. |
School field trips—Fiction. | Amusement parks—Fiction. | Stealing—
Fiction. | Plot-your-own stories. | GSAFD: Mystery fiction. |
LCGFT: Detective and mystery fiction.
Classification: LCC PZ7.B7576 Cac 2017 | DDC 813.6 [Fic] — dc23
LC record available at https://lccn.loc.gov/2016040634

Graphic Designer: Kristi Carlson
Editor: Megan Atwood
Production Artist: Laura Manthe

Summary: After electronic cards for rides and games go missing from a
carnival during a field trip, junior detectives Sam, Egg, Gum, and Cat are
on the case!

Printed in Canada.
010050S17

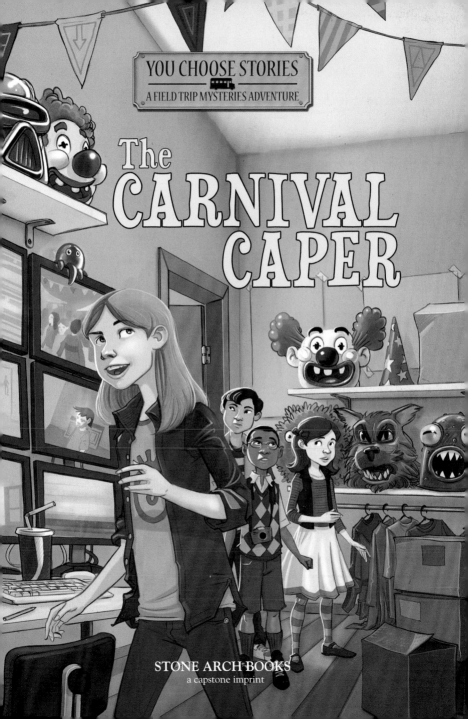

YOU CHOOSE STORIES
A FIELD TRIP MYSTERIES ADVENTURE

The CARNIVAL CAPER

STONE ARCH BOOKS
a capstone imprint

Catalina Duran

A.K.A.: Cat

BIRTHDAY: February 15th

LEVEL: 6th Grade

INTERESTS:

Animals, being "green,"
field trips

Edward G. Garrison

A.K.A.: Egg

BIRTHDAY: May 14th

LEVEL: 6th Grade

INTERESTS:

Photography, field trips

James Shoo

A.K.A.: Gum

BIRTHDAY: November 19th

LEVEL: 6th Grade

INTERESTS:

Gum-chewing, field trips, and showing everyone what a crook Anton Gutman is

Samantha Archer

A.K.A.: Sam

BIRTHDAY: August 20th

LEVEL: 6th Grade

INTERESTS:

Old movies, field trips

FIELD TRIP MYSTERIES

"You guys," Samantha Archer says. She grabs hold of the seatback in front of her and leans over a little.

In front of her sit James "Gum" Shoo and Catalina Duran, two of her best friends. The third, Edward "Egg" Garrison, sits next to her.

"This is it," Sam says. "This is the big one: Wackyville Carnival and Fun Zone. The biggest trip of sixth grade."

Gum twists in the seat and blows a big pink bubble. Cat backs away just before it pops and Gum expertly pulls it back into his mouth to keep chewing.

"You don't have to remind me," Gum says. "I've been counting the days since kindergarten."

"Really?" Egg says, popping his head up. "Because that's . . . over two thousand days."

TURN THE PAGE.

"It's an expression," Gum says, dropping back into his seat as the bus pulls into the big Wackyville parking lot.

It takes three buses to haul the entire sixth grade from Franklin Middle School to the amusement park for the day. They pull into the bus parking area. The brakes hiss and thunk.

The doors seem to sigh as they open. The sixth graders all but burst from the buses.

"I can't wait to hit the midway where the games are," Gum says. "I plan to win enough tickets to bring home that ZCube game system."

"Not me," Sam says, rubbing her hands together. "They've got the oldest wooden roller coaster in the state. I'm gonna ride it fifty times."

"Just fifty?" Cat says, elbowing Egg and winking at him.

"Maybe a hundred!" Sam says.

The four friends hurry along with their classmates as their teachers and parent-chaperones do their best to herd the kids toward the amusement park's main gates.

When they reach the front gate, though, it's been pulled down as if the park is closed. Standing in front of it is a park security guard and a man in tan pants and a wrinkled orange shirt.

Their teacher, Mr. Spade, is already at the gate. He'd taken his own car to meet them here.

"What the heckle?" Cat says.

"What's going on?" asks Mr. Spade.

Cat, Gum, Egg, and Sam gather around him, snooping as usual.

"I'm Mr. Dawson, the park manager," says the man in the tan suit. "And it's rather embarrassing, actually. In fact, we'd close for the day if not for your field trip. We tried to call but you were already on your way."

"What's happened?" Mr. Spade says.

"An entire case of our specially printed plastic cards with the magnetic strips has gone missing," Mr. Dawson says. "Right out of the main office here at the park."

"Stolen?!" Sam and Egg say at the same time.

TURN THE PAGE.

Mr. Dawson laughs nervously. "We're not jumping to any conclusions!" he says, forcing a smile. "But it *is* a problem."

"Those are the cards visitors use to pay for rides?" Mr. Spade asks.

"And games, meals, and souvenirs," Mr. Dawson says, nodding. "They even keep track of how many tickets visitors have won on the midway!"

"No more paper tickets?" Mr. Spade asks.

"We did away with those several months ago," Mr. Dawson says. "Litter everywhere. The tickets were damp with sweat by the time visitors turned them in!"

"I see," Mr. Spade says. "So the cards are quite valuable."

"Not at all, actually," Mr. Dawson says, "until *we* scan them and add money or prizes. The missing carton of blank cards is nearly worthless, but without them, we can't do a thing!"

"What?" Sam says. "No rides?"

"No prize tickets?" Gum says.

Mr. Dawson shakes his head. "I'm afraid not," he says. "Everything in the park is linked through the computer system, and it all depends on those cards to work."

"Everything?" Mr. Spade asks.

"Pretty much," Mr. Dawson says.

He nods to the guard, who pulls up the gate. It thunders as it rolls into its metal case above them.

"Oh," Mr. Dawson says quickly, almost as an afterthought. "There is mini-golf. That doesn't require a computer to run. The staff will hand out balls and clubs — as many as you need. Play as much as you like!"

"Now what?" Cat asks her best friends quietly as they huddle together. Around the four junior detectives, the whole sixth grade rushes in.

"It's a case," Sam says, shoving her hands into her pockets. "We solve it."

"But how?" Egg says.

TO PLAY A ROUND OF MINI-GOLF AND LOOK FOR CLUES, TURN TO PAGE 12.
TO SNOOP AROUND THE PARK FOR ANSWERS, TURN TO PAGE 14.
TO GO DIRECTLY TO THE OFFICE TO LOOK FOR PHYSICAL EVIDENCE, TURN TO PAGE 16.

"I have a theory," Gum says. He's got one eye closed tight as he lines up his putt on a par three. It's his tenth putt.

"About the crime?" Sam says.

"About *a* crime," Gum says. He taps the ball; it zips right past the hole and off the green. "This *game* is a crime. A crime of *boredom*."

Cat giggles. "Oh, come on," she says as she steps up to take her putt. "It's kinda fun, I think."

Cat taps her yellow ball. It rolls into the cup.

"Hole in two," she announces as she picks up her ball.

"After eleven holes," Egg says, scratching sums on the scorecard, "Cat is winning with . . . four under par."

"It's a crime because the people who stink the most," Gum says as he tries the putt once more, "end up playing the longest!"

Mr. Spade walks by, his club on his shoulder and a bright orange ball in his hand. "Don't be so discouraged, James!" he says.

"I'm not," Gum says. "I'd have to care to be discouraged."

Mr. Spade laughs. "Mini-golf is a fascinating sport," he says, getting down on one knee. "It's got math, geometry, physics . . ."

"Everything I look for in a sport," Gum says under his breath.

"You have to think about angles and force," he says. "It's very exciting."

He stands. "In a way, the missing cards are a blessing," he says, grinning. "As much mini-golf as we like. What a day!"

Still smiling, he troops off, back toward hole number one to play through again.

"Guys," Sam says. "Are you thinking what I'm thinking?"

"Yeah," Gum says. "Mr. Spade is a nut."

"No," Sam says. "Well, yeah. But I mean, I think Mr. Spade is our prime suspect!"

To find physical evidence to support this theory, turn to page 18.

To question the other teachers and chaperones to gather evidence against Mr. Spade, turn to page 25.

"I don't get why they don't just let us go on all the rides we want," Gum says, as he and his friends stroll past a roller coaster. "It's not *our* fault the cards are missing."

He grabs hold of the closed steel gate blocking entry to the roller coaster and gives it a tug. It won't budge.

"They're locked," Sam says, "and they only unlock for a working card."

"There must be a way to bypass that," Egg says. "Don't they have to test the rides sometimes?"

"The park would probably get in big trouble if they let us ride like that," Cat says.

They walk through the midway, normally full of carnival games, food vendors, and performers in costumes and on stilts. Today, though, the booths are all shuttered.

In fact, the place is deserted — aside from a picnic table tucked off into the corner of the midway.

There, a young woman in a park employee uniform sits, her elbows on the table, her head low over a thick textbook and a spiral notebook.

"I guess she gets an easy day today," Cat says. "Nice day to study outside."

Sam nods and scribbles something in the little notebook she always keeps in her back pocket.

The four sleuths move on to the far side of the midway. There, thick as thieves tucked away behind a restroom outbuilding, are Anton and his two henchmen, Luca and Hans.

"What are they up to?" Gum says.

"Nothing good," Cat says, glowering, "as usual."

"We should find out," Egg says. He snaps a few photos of the conspiring sixth graders.

Sam shakes her head. "Let's chat with that woman back there," she says. "Free day off to study for the big test. Maybe she made it happen."

To question the employee who is studying, turn to page 20.
To tail Anton, Luca, and Hans, turn to page 27.

Sam strides up to the ticket booth. "Excuse me, can you tell us where the office is?"

"The main office?" says the young woman in the ticket booth. "It's around back. I don't think anyone's there right now, though."

"Thanks," Sam says. But the woman in the booth doesn't even look up from her phone.

The four sleuths move to the office door. "Should we knock?" Egg asks.

"Good thinking," Sam says. "If someone answers, we make an excuse. Otherwise we know the coast is clear."

She knocks, but nothing happens.

Sam leads the sleuths inside. A cat leaps out of the corner and lands right on Sam's arm.

"Ah!" Sam shouts, dropping the cat to the floor.

It lands on its feet and rubs its face against Sam's ankle.

Sam sneezes.

"Get it away from me!" she says, her nose closing up and her eyes going red. "I'm very allergic!"

Cat scoops up the cat. "Oh, poor thing," she says. "Look, he's only got one eye. Aw."

"Gross," Gum says. "Or, pirate!"

Cat clicks her tongue at him.

While she and Gum scratch the cat's ears and let him grab at a pen they take from a desk near the door, Egg and Sam check the office over for clues.

"Okay, Mr. Dawson," comes the voice of the woman in the booth. "I'll take care of it."

The door to the ticket booth begins to open.

"Quick!" Sam hisses to her friends. "Skedaddle!"

The sleuths hurry from the office just before the young woman opens the door all the way — just in time to see the main door close.

"Now what?" Egg says when the four detectives are far enough away from the office.

"I didn't find anything in there," Sam says.

She sneezes.

"Except *dander*," she adds.

To question employees of the park, turn to page 23.
To question other sixth graders, turn to page 29.

"The first thing we should do," Sam says, leading her friends to begin the investigation, "is see if there's any surveillance footage."

The four friends approach the ticket counter near the park's main gate. Behind the windows, a young employee sits on a stool, staring at her phone.

"Hi," Sam says.

The young woman doesn't even look up.

"Park's closed," she says, "except for a field trip."

"Oh, we know," Egg says. "We're with the field trip."

"So go play mini-golf," she says.

"We were wondering," Sam says. "No one's found the missing cards yet, right?"

"Nope," she says, tapping her phone.

Just then, Mr. Dawson steps into the ticket booth through a back door. "Is there anything I can help you with?" he asks. He seems annoyed.

"What's his problem?" Gum whispers to Sam.

"Sir," Cat says, "is there any surveillance footage from this morning?"

Mr. Dawson's mouth tightens. He replies with his eyebrows high. "I'm afraid not," he says. "Our cameras don't record. They only allow us to watch the park from a central location."

"Maybe you should upgrade the surveillance to digital," Egg says, "like you have the tickets."

"Maybe we should," Mr. Dawson grumbles.

"When did you last see the cards?" Sam asks, leaning into the ticket window a little.

"I haven't the foggiest," Mr. Dawson says. "Now, if you'll excuse me — "

"I know this one," says the young woman on the stool. "I received the shipment before locking up last night. I put the carton in the office."

Mr. Dawson scowls at her, but she doesn't notice. She keeps looking at her phone, smiling.

Mr. Dawson turns his scowl on the kids. "Why are you four asking so many questions?"

"No reason," Egg says, pulling his friends away. "Gotta go!"

To sneak into the office to look for clues, turn to page 32.
To check Mr. Spade's car in the parking lot, turn to page 48.

Sam leads her friends back to the midway.

"Follow my lead," Sam says.

Sam sits right down at the young woman's table, directly across from her. "Hi," Sam says.

Her friends flank Sam and wait.

The young woman looks up. They can see the name tag on her chest: Ana.

She looks at Sam for a moment, then sighs the most tortured sigh the friends have ever heard.

""We just want to talk for a second," Cat says, giving Ana her most winning smile. It doesn't work.

"What?" Ana says. "Why?"

"I assume you've heard about the missing cards," Sam says, leaning toward Ana.

"Obviously," Ana says. "That's why I'm studying instead of working."

"You run one of the booths?" Sam says.

"Yeah," Ana says.

"Taking the local cake-eaters' dough?" Sam says, her voice rising.

TURN TO PAGE 22.

"What?" Ana says.

"Needed the morning off today, though, huh?" Sam goes on. "Figured you'd finger a stack, shutter the fence-to-fence?"

Ana stares at her for a moment. "Why do you talk like that?" she asks.

"She just means you're probably glad the midway is closed today," Gum says.

"I do have a test tonight," Ana says, "and I have to study. It's hard to find the time."

"Big test?" Cat asks sympathetically.

Ana nods. "Astronomy final," she says. "If I don't pass, I don't graduate."

"Ooh, astronomy," Egg says, sliding closer to Ana on the bench. "Maybe I can help?"

Ana looks down her nose at Egg and scoffs. Then she sneezes, and moves to a different table.

"She's got to be the crook," Sam says.

"But we need some evidence," Egg says.

TO FIND THE MANAGER AND ACCUSE ANA, TURN TO PAGE 34.
TO FIND PHYSICAL EVIDENCE PROVING ANA'S GUILT, TURN TO PAGE 52.

The sleuths walk to the mini-golf course. Sam sidles up to the mini-golf counter and leans against it. She says to the man working behind the counter, "Not many employees around today."

The man says, "I guess."

"So where is everyone?" Cat asks.

He shrugs. "Break room, probably," he says. "Over in the big building across the plaza. Meanwhile I'm stuck on mini-golf duty."

"Yeah, tough break," Sam says. She leads her friends toward the building across the plaza.

Once in the building, they hear the low murmur of conversation from up the hallway. Soon they reach an open door, and inside is a large kitchen with two circular tables in the middle.

Both tables are full of park employees. They all look up at the four kids standing in the doorway.

"Aren't you kids from the field trip?" one of them asks.

The detectives nod as they move into the break room.

"Aren't you supposed to be playing mini-golf?" asks a man with a beard. His name tag says Eugene.

"We got bored," Gum says.

"Fair enough," says Eugene.

Then he sneezes.

"Allergies?" Sam asks. "That cat in the office made me sneeze like crazy."

"No, I'm not allergic," says Eugene. "I just have a cold. But if I take another sick day, I won't be able to pay my rent. That's why I've been trying to get everyone to strike." He smiles a crooked smile. "It's not exactly a sick day, but no one can work! Looks like I got a sit-in after all." Eugene laughs, but no one joins him.

The sleuths turn to leave and Sam says quietly, "Eugene is definitely a suspect. The cards are gone and he got his strike." She shrugs. "Kind of."

"We ought to snoop around this building," Gum says. "I bet there are plenty of places to stash the stolen goods."

To tell Mr. Dawson that Eugene has a strong motive, turn to page 36.
To snoop around the building to find clues, turn to page 55.

Gum, Sam, Egg, and Cat stroll away from the mini-golf course.

"Giving up already?" Mr. Spade calls after them.

"Hardly," Sam says quietly. "Let's find out what Mr. Spade did this morning before we got here."

Soon they find Ms. Pagalucci, another sixth-grade teacher. She sits on a bench and sips coffee from a travel mug.

"Hey, Ms. P.," Sam says, sitting next to her.

Ms. P. is well known as the friendliest and coolest sixth-grade teacher at Franklin Middle School.

"Sam," she says. She smiles at the others. "Hi, Gum. Egg. Cat."

Ms. P. is also the only person on staff at Franklin who uses the sleuths' nicknames.

"Having any fun so far?" Ms. P. asks.

"I won at mini-golf," Cat says.

"Nice!" Ms. P. says, giving Cat a high five. "That sounds fun. As for me, I prefer coffee to mini-golf."

TURN THE PAGE.

"I was wondering," Sam says. "Why did Mr. Spade take his car to Wackyville instead of the bus?"

Ms. P. sips her coffee and furrows her brow at Sam. Then she says, "He insisted on coming down here before the buses."

"Is that . . . odd?" Cat asks.

Ms. P. shrugs. "What do I know?" she says. "It's only my second year teaching. But if you ask me, everything that man does is odd." She winks at the kids.

With that, she knocks back the last few drops of her coffee. "I'm going to find a refill," she says as she stands. "See you kids later."

"So he has motive," Egg says, "and now he has opportunity, since he was at the park long before anyone else."

"Then we've got him nailed," Sam says. "Let's bust him."

"I don't know," Cat says. "This is Mr. Spade. Let's talk to someone else first to be sure."

To interview another sixth-grade teacher or chaperone, turn to page 68.

To accuse Mr. Spade, turn to page 86.

Gum, Egg, Cat, and Sam follow Anton and his friends along the winding paths of the amusement park.

The trio of troublemakers look over their shoulders a few times as they walk, but the sleuths are careful. Anton and the goons never spot them.

They walk deeper into the amusement park, along wooded paths. They pass signs that say *TO AMPHITHEATER* and *TO SOUTH EXIT*.

"Where are they going?" Cat whispers. "There's nothing to see way down there."

"They're up to something," Sam says.

"They're probably just looking for a place to write their names in marker," Egg says. The sleuths have caught Anton, Luca, and Hans writing graffiti in marker on field trips in the past.

"I always forget," Gum says, "that those three even know how to write."

Eventually, Anton and his friends seem satisfied with how far from the rest of the students they've gotten.

TURN THE PAGE.

The trio steps into a cluster of trees just off the path.

Sam, Gum, Egg, and Cat crouch behind a hedge that runs along the path. From there, they can see all three vandals, though they can't quite hear them.

Anton, grinning like a cat that's just found a mouse, pulls a folded white envelope from his back pocket. He slips it open.

And he pulls out a thick stack of plastic cards.

"He has the cards!" Gum says, almost too loud.

Cat shushes him.

"Let's bust them!" Gum says. "They're really guilty this time!"

Cat hums nervously. "We should get Mr. Spade," Cat says. "Or Mr. Dawson, the manager. Or both."

"They're like ten miles from here!" Gum says.

Egg snaps a few photos of the troublemakers. "I think Cat's right," Egg says.

The three look at Sam to choose.

To bust Anton and his goons right here, turn to page 71.
To get adult help, turn to page 89.

The four friends split up to roam the mini-golf course and talk to their classmates.

Most of the sixth graders are bored with mini-golf by now, but no one has any good info about the crime.

"That was a waste of time," Sam says when the friends reunite at the eighteenth hole.

"I nearly had to take another golf club when Mr. Spade found me at the eleventh hole," Gum says, shivering.

Cat nods. "Between the four of us, I think we talked to the whole sixth grade," she says.

Egg looks past her, farther into the park. "Not everyone," he says. "Look."

His friends quickly spot a blue-haired girl sitting on a bench with a big sketchpad on her lap, drawing away.

"Chloe Marshfield," Sam says, lowering her gaze. "Come on."

They hurry along the winding path to the bench where Chloe is sitting, facing the big Ferris wheel.

TURN THE PAGE.

A big shoulder bag sits on the ground beside her.

"This," she says as soon as the four sleuths arrive, "is tough to sketch. But fun. The angles, the perspective, the shapes. Really challenging."

"Chloe," Sam says, "have you seen anything suspicious at the park this morning?"

"Not really," Chloe says. "Just you four snooping around, as usual."

Cat frowns at her.

"Oh," Chloe says, finally taking her eyes off her work. "I did see Anton and those two big boys he hangs out with. They ran off to the other side of the park. They seemed pretty suspicious."

"Thanks, Chloe," Egg says.

"I mean, they always look suspicious, though, right?" Chloe adds as the four sleuths head off. "Hey, you guys always do too, come to think of it!"

"So we go find Anton, right?" Gum says.

"We should also question the chaperones," Sam says. "They're all hanging around too."

To find Anton and his friends, turn to page 73.
To question the chaperones, turn to page 92.

"There's the office," Sam says.

She and her friends crouch behind some recycling cans across the walkway from the rear of the ticket booth.

A plain gray door is the only thing that breaks the tan, cement wall.

"How do we get in?" Gum says.

"Good question," Egg says. "We know Mr. Dawson is in there."

Just then, the door opens.

The four sleuths duck lower in their hiding spot.

Mr. Dawson emerges and walks away from the office. When he's out of sight around the corner, the children stand up.

"Let's go," Sam says, starting toward the door.

"Wait!" Cat says, grabbing Sam's wrist. "What about the woman in the ticket booth?"

"Her?" Sam says. "Don't be silly. She's not moving unless the building's on fire."

The four hurry across the walkway to the door.

Sam tries the handle. "It's open," she says. "This is too easy."

They slip inside and close the door quietly behind them.

The office is small and cluttered. There are a dozen file cabinets, a bank of black-and-white monitors for the surveillance cameras, and three metal desks that don't match each other.

There's a door on the far wall. "That must lead to the ticket booth," Sam says.

There's another door on the wall to their left. It's marked *Restroom*. It stands open slightly.

"Let's keep quiet and look around," Sam says as she moves deeper into the room. Egg and Gum fan out behind her.

"What are we looking for?" Cat says, still standing by the entrance.

"Well, we can't dust for fingerprints," Sam admits, "but maybe something will leap out at us."

Egg takes a few photos. "Never know what we might find in one of these shots later," Egg says.

TURN TO PAGE 38.

The kids hurry through the midway to the office located around the back of the ticket booth.

Sam thumps the plain gray door with the side of her fist. "Anyone in there?" she shouts.

The door opens to a confused Mr. Dawson. "Yes?" he says.

"We think we know who stole the missing cards!" Sam announces.

His eyebrows go up. "You do, do you?" he asks.

"Ana," Sam says. "She's one of your employees."

"Ana?" Mr. Dawson says. "I've never had any trouble with her."

"We saw her studying," Cat explains. "It seems like having the day off is just what she needed."

"Now that you mention it," Mr. Dawson says, "she did ask for the day off today. Something about a big test tonight."

He chuckles. "I guess she got the day off anyway," he says. "You saw her studying and put that together, huh?"

Sam starts to smile, but suddenly her face twists, clenches, and explodes with a sneeze.

"Bless you!" Mr. Dawson says.

"Excuse me," Sam says. "Have you got a cat in there? Because I'm aller — " She sneezes again, making everyone jump.

As if on cue, a dark gray cat leaps out of the office and into Mr. Dawson's arms.

"This is Coal," he says. "He was a stray, but we took him in."

"He's very friendly," Cat says. She gives Coal a little scratch on the forehead. He purrs and presses his head against her hand.

"All right, Coaly," Mr. Dawson coos to the cat. He sets him down in the doorway and gives him a pet. "I'll be right back."

With that, Mr. Dawson closes the door to the office, leaving Coal behind. "I'll just have a look in Ana's locker," he says to the sleuths as he pulls out his keychain. "I have a key to every employee locker."

TURN TO PAGE 42.

The kids walk to the office, and just as they arrive, the office door flies open.

"Whoa!" Sam says, just dodging the door.

"Oh, goodness!" says Mr. Dawson, standing in the open doorway. "I'm so sorry. Did I get you?"

"No, but it was close," Sam says, rubbing her nose as if it had been hit.

"What a *day*," Mr. Dawson says.

"Speaking of that," Sam says, "we were talking to some of the park employees, and it seems Eugene has a motive to steal the cards."

Mr. Dawson looks at the sleuths and says, "Yes, he's a troublemaker, all right. But what good would it do him to steal the cards?"

"He's been trying to organize your employees for better wages," Egg explains.

Mr. Dawson thinks it over. "That wouldn't make sense," he says. "If the management doesn't know about the strike, then it's not a strike. But Eugene isn't one to think things through, I suppose."

He sighs deeply. "Anyway," he says. "I don't get paid near enough myself. Those kids in the break room ought to try working at the park when they have a mortgage and a family to support like I do."

Cat and Egg exchange a glance.

Mr. Dawson sighs. "Listen," he says, leaning in the doorway. "No one who works here is paid enough. I think those blasted cards are partially to blame, in fact."

"How do you mean?" Sam says.

"Apparently," Mr. Dawson says, "computer hackers and rip-off artists have an easy time fooling the card readers.

"They're able to input false information onto their magnetic strips," Mr. Dawson goes on, "and to convince the computers here at the park that they've won millions of prize tickets, or deposited thousands of dollars in cash on their cards."

Sam nods. "I see," she says. "Then the cards aren't entirely worthless, are they?"

TURN TO PAGE 45.

Gum pulls open a mini-fridge. "Nothing interesting in here," he says.

"What did you think you'd find in there that has anything to do with the crime?" Cat asks.

"Who said anything about the crime?" Gum says. "I was just hoping for a snack."

"I'm not finding anything useful," Sam says. She's standing on her tiptoes on top of a box of printer paper, trying to look on the highest shelves.

At the same moment, a loud crash comes from behind the bathroom door.

"Uh-oh," Gum says. "Someone's here!"

From across the room, Sam shushes him.

Egg crouches next to a file cabinet.

The restroom door creaks as it opens more.

With no chance of escaping unnoticed now, the four friends stand still, barely breathing, as they watch the door open farther and farther.

When it's open fully, no one's there. Only a small night-light glows inside the restroom.

"What gives?" Gum says.

The four friends gather in the middle of the small office. They move together toward the door.

"Is this a *haunted* carnival?" Cat whispers.

Soon they stand in the open doorway and look into the empty bathroom.

A dark little figure leaps from the dim bathroom, snarling and mewing. It bounds off Sam's shoulder.

Sam screams.

Cat shrieks.

Egg starts snapping pictures.

And the thing lands on the desk behind them.

"Oh!" Cat says. "It's a kitty!"

Indeed, staring back at the four detectives is a dark gray, lean cat with big ears and only one working eye. It hisses.

Sam sneezes. "I'm outta here!" she announces, snatching a tissue and then running from the office.

She shoves the office door open — right into Mr. Dawson.

TURN TO PAGE 41.

"Oh, excuse me," Sam says. "I can explain." But before she can even try, she sneezes again.

"What is the meaning of this?!" Mr. Dawson shouts, his face going red with anger.

Gum, Cat, and Egg hurry out after Sam, but the damage is done.

Mr. Spade hurries over, his golf club still in his hand. "What's wrong, Mr. Dawson?"

Then he sees the four sleuths, and his face falls. "Don't tell me," he says. "These four have been snooping around."

"It appears so, yes," Mr. Dawson says.

Mr. Spade puts his fists on his hips. "You four know the drill," he says. "Let's go."

The four friends follow after Mr. Spade back to the parking lot and onto the bus.

"Honestly, kids," Mr. Spade says as they climb aboard. "If this keeps happening, we'll have to stop inviting you on field trips!"

THE END

TO FOLLOW ANOTHER PATH, TURN TO PAGE 11.

The kids follow Mr. Dawson across a plaza to a tan building. He leads them inside through a door marked *EMPLOYEES ONLY* and then along a plain-looking, chilly hallway.

Mr. Dawson leads them into the employee locker room. "I'm not sure Mr. Spade would like you tagging along," he says, one eyebrow up. "But . . . it was your idea."

He finds Ana's locker — number 42 — and uses his key on the combination lock. It opens with a thunk. "Nothing."

"Nothing?" Sam says, shocked. But all that's there is a T-shirt, a pair of jeans, and a purse.

"So unless Ana stashed them someplace else," Mr. Dawson says, "I think she's off the hook."

"Just a second," Cat says. "I have an idea."

She turns to Mr. Dawson. "First I need something from you."

Ten minutes later, with a walkie-talkie in her shoulder bag and permission from Mr. Dawson, Cat leads her friends back to the midway.

They find Ana still studying. She sneezes just as they arrive.

"Bless you," Cat says, smiling.

Ana is startled. "Oh," she says. "It's you again."

Cat says, "We were just saying we hope your cold clears up by tonight so you can concentrate."

"I don't have a cold," Ana says, looking back at her work.

"Allergies, huh?" Sam says. She leans over and picks something off of Ana's uniform. She holds up her fingers and says, "A coal-gray hair from a coal-gray cat."

"Do you work in the office, Ana?" Cat asks.

"No," Ana says. "I work on the midway. I never go in the office."

"Except first thing this morning, right?" Sam says. "And a coal-gray cat rubbed against you." Sam laughs and adds, "Doesn't it seem like cats *know* who has allergies?"

TURN THE PAGE.

"Fine, yes! I went into the office this morning!" she says. "I was in there for like ten seconds — "

"You went to the office to steal cards," Cat says.

Suddenly the walkie-talkie in Cat's bag crackles to life: "I'm reading you loud and clear."

Ana's eyes go wide. "Mr. Dawson!" she says. "I didn't steal the cards. I just sort of . . . hid them. I'll show you where they are."

Ana packs her stuff and runs toward the office.

Gum pats Cat on the back. "That was top-notch detective work," he says.

"Thanks," Cat says, her cheeks going red.

"And now the rides will work here," Egg says.

"But thievery won't!" Gum yells, smiling triumphantly. But all he sees are confused looks. "Work here, I mean. Thievery won't work here."

Cat pats him on the shoulder. "Sure, Gum," she says. "Let's go ride some rides."

THE END

TO FOLLOW ANOTHER PATH, TURN TO PAGE 11.

Mr. Dawson bites his lip. "No," he admits. "At least, not necessarily."

"What does that have to do with the park workers not getting paid well?" Egg asks.

"We've lost money on the dumb things!" Mr. Dawson says. "First there was all the new equipment and computers. Then there were the scammers. It's hit us hard."

"So, go back to paper tickets!" Gum says.

"I would," Mr. Dawson says, "but the folks at headquarters won't allow it."

He glances at his watch. "Excuse me, kids," he says, pulling the door behind him. "I have to run. Have fun."

With that, he rushes away.

"I wish we could snoop around in there a bit more," Gum says.

"No prob," Sam says, pulling the door open.

"He didn't lock it?" Egg says.

"He didn't even close it," Sam says. "I blocked it with my toe. Come on."

TURN THE PAGE.

Sam stays close to the door and covers her nose. "I'll stay here," she says, "and try to avoid the cat."

Coal prowls the office, finally climbing to the highest shelf.

Then he starts meowing. Loudly.

"Shh!" Cat hisses up at the cat.

But he meows even louder as he paces.

"What's going on in here?" the employee says as she throws open the door from the ticket booth.

At the same moment, the metal door opens and Mr. Dawson comes in, a worried look on his face. "What's the meaning of this?" he says.

Mr. Spade is right behind Mr. Dawson.

"We can explain!" Gum says.

"Don't bother," Mr. Spade says. "The four of you, come with me. You'll be spending the rest of this trip on the b — "

Just then, Coal leaps down from the shelf, taking a couple of cardboard file boxes with him.

One of them tumbles to the floor. Its contents spill all over the rug: thousands of plastic cards with magnetic strips on one side and the Wackyville logo on the other.

"Well, here they are! Someone must have misplaced them!" Mr. Dawson says, gathering the cards and laughing awkwardly.

He pushes the sleuths and Mr. Spade out of the office. A bead of sweat drips down his temple. "Nothing to see here. Thank you!" He slams the metal door in their faces.

"He hates those cards!" Cat says.

"He told us himself!" Gum says.

"I'm sure he simply mislaid them," Mr. Spade says. "Now let's get ready for some rides!"

He heads off to tell the class the good news.

Cat shrugs. "I guess this is a happy ending."

"I guess," Sam says. "We can't prove our criminal is the criminal. But at least we don't have to stay on the bus this trip!"

THE END

TO FOLLOW ANOTHER PATH, TURN TO PAGE 11.

Sam, Egg, Cat, and Gum crouch behind a big shrub cut into a rectangle. From there, they can see the park's front gate.

"One park guard," Sam whispers as she pokes her head up to look over the hedge. "And Ms. Marco."

Ms. Marco is a classmate's mom and a chaperone for the trip.

"We can't let her see us," Egg says. "She won't let us go to the parking lot by ourselves."

"Maybe we can tell her we left something on the bus?" Cat suggests.

"Then she'd escort us to the bus," Sam says. "We have to get to Mr. Spade's car."

"I got this," Gum says. "Wait for my signal."

"What are you going to do?" Cat asks.

"Trust me!" Gum says in a voice that makes Cat, Egg, and Sam trust him just a little less.

Gum struts out from behind the hedge. "Hey, Ms. Marco!" he shouts. "Can you help me?"

"Oh!" Ms. Marco says. "James Shoo, what are you doing over here?"

"I got lost," Gum says.

Ms. Marco puts a comforting hand on Gum's shoulder. "The mini-golf is nowhere near here, James," she says. "Why'd you wander so far?"

"I was looking for my ball," Gum says. "Can you help me find my way back to mini-golf?"

Ms. Marco smiles nervously at the guards before she says to Gum, "I'm not sure I know the way. This place is so big."

"Oh, I'll be happy to show you both," the guard says, adjusting his cap. "Follow me."

"Thanks!" Gum says.

He follows behind Ms. Marco as the security guard leads them back toward the mini-golf course. As they pass the hedge, Gum gives his friends a thumbs-up without Ms. Marco noticing.

"I guess that's the signal," Sam says. "Let's go."

TURN THE PAGE.

"He hates mini-golf," Cat says as they creep out from behind the hedge. "He sacrificed himself so we could solve the case."

"What a hero," Egg says, rolling his eyes.

"We should hurry," Sam says. "The guard will be back soon."

Since the park is mostly closed today, there aren't many cars in the lot. They spot Mr. Spade's pretty quickly: it's parked on the northern edge, the only part of the lot with shade — and a five-minute walk from the gate.

Sam takes a deep breath. "Come on," she says, and starts running toward his car.

Egg and Cat hurry along behind her. Neither can quite keep up.

"In a way," Egg says, "it's a good thing Gum sacrificed himself."

Cat laughs, a little out of breath. "Yeah," she says. "He hates running more than any of us."

Turn to page 58.

"How will we find any evidence in a place this size?" Egg says, throwing up his arms — either to show how big the park is or how hopeless the case is.

"That's a good point," Gum says. "It's not like we can dust all of Wackyville for fingerprints."

"Or walk every path," Cat says, squinting and miming a magnifying glass to her eye, "checking for footprints."

Egg and Gum laugh.

Sam puts an arm around Cat. "We don't need to check the whole place, guys," she says. "Just the spots that make sense."

"Like wherever they keep the plastic cards," Egg says.

Sam taps her nose.

"Or where the employees keep their stuff!" Cat says.

Sam smiles. "I like the way you two are thinking," she says. "Let's see what we can find."

Their first stop is the ticket window at the front of the park. Inside, a bored-looking employee sits on a high stool, scrolling through her phone and popping bubbles.

The tag on her shirt reads Carlotta.

"Let me handle this," Sam says quietly to her friends. "I have a hunch."

Sam says to Carlotta in the ticket booth, "It's my first day today."

"Good for you," Carlotta says without looking up.

"Mr. Dawson didn't tell me where to put my stuff," Sam says.

With her eyes still on her phone, Carlotta raises one hand and points at the building behind the kids, across the plaza. "Employee locker room, in there."

"Great, thanks," Sam says, backing quickly away from the window. To her friends, she says, "Come on." The kids cross the plaza and pull open a pair of glass doors marked *EMPLOYEES ONLY*. Beyond is a quiet hallway leading deep into the building.

TURN THE PAGE.

The kids stick their heads inside room after room until they finally find a room of metal lockers.

"Which one is Ana's?" Cat asks as the four kids stand there in the center of the locker room. "They're not marked."

"They're all numbered," Gum points out. "What's her number?"

"How should I know?" Cat says.

Just then, footsteps ring out from the hallway. "You guys," Sam hisses. "Hide. Quick."

Cat and Sam take a shower stall. Gum slips into a closet, leaving the door ajar. Egg, running out of time and options, finds a locker with no lock and jumps inside.

And not a moment too soon. Through the slats, Egg sees Ana walk into the room.

She strolls up to a locker across from him but farther along the row. She twists the combination lock, pulls it open, and opens the locker.

TURN TO PAGE 62.

Gum leads his friends to a room full of lockers.

"The employee locker room," Sam says. "This could work."

"One problem, though," Egg says, tugging on a padlock. "They're all locked."

"Aw, man!" Gum says.

"Well, it was worth a shot," Sam says. "And it's no reason we have to give up now. The crook could have stashed those cards anywhere in this building."

The four friends move deeper into the staff building.

They try every door handle and peek into every open room, but they find nothing.

The girls' restroom sign comes into view and Sam says, "Wait here. I need to make a stop."

She hurries into the bathroom. Another door inside the room catches her attention: the janitor's closet.

Inside, there are a couple of mops, some shelves full of cleaning supplies . . . and a slim, white cardboard box tucked away behind a bottle of bleach.

TURN THE PAGE.

Sam pushes the cleaning supplies aside and pulls down the cardboard box. She slips off the top.

"The cards," she whispers, then bursts out of the bathroom. "I found them!" she says.

She presents the uncovered box to her friends, who grin in surprise.

"We have to get these to Mr. Dawson," Sam says.

The four friends burst out of the building onto the sunny plaza. "Mr. Dawson!" Sam shouts gleefully as they run. "Mr. Dawson!"

Mr. Dawson comes out from behind the ticket booth. "What is it?" he asks.

Mr. Spade appears from the direction of the mini-golf course.

"Good news!" Sam shouts.

"We found the cards!" Gum says.

Mr. Dawson's jaw drops. Mr. Spade smiles. The two men arrive at the ticket window just as the four friends skid to a stop. Sam holds out the box.

"Well," Mr. Spade says. "I'm impressed."

Mr. Dawson accepts the box and pulls off the lid. "Where did you find them?" he asks, looking at Sam.

Sam tells him, and Mr. Dawson clicks his tongue.

"You're not supposed to be in there," he says. "That building is for staff."

Cat says, "We were investigating the crime — and the employees inside didn't seem to mind."

Mr. Dawson sighs. "But we have no idea who took the cards," he says.

Sam sneezes.

"That reminds me," Cat says. "I have an idea about how we can find out."

Fifteen minutes later, the sleuths, Mr. Spade, and Mr. Dawson stand outside the break room and talk quietly.

"I hope you're right about this," Mr. Dawson says.

"It'll work," Cat says to Mr. Dawson and her friends. "Most of the staff never go into the office, right?"

"Right," Mr. Dawson says.

Turn to page 65.

Mr. Spade's car is a forest-green station wagon. The passenger-side window is broken and only closes halfway, so the top part is covered in a thick plastic sheet, held in place with shiny silver duct tape.

"Boy," Sam says, looking the car over with her hands on her hips. "Teachers *really* don't get paid enough."

The inside is a total mess: papers, books, an old sport coat — even a couple of golf putters. "He sure loves mini-golf," Sam mutters to herself.

"But that's not evidence," Egg says.

Sam nods. "You're right," she says, "and if there's a carton of plastic cards in there somewhere, I don't see it."

"Plus, the doors are locked," Cat points out.

"This is a bust," Sam says. "We'd better get back before we're — "

Before she can finish, though, Egg interrupts. "Uh-oh," he says, looking past her.

Sam looks over her shoulder.

Almost silently, a park security guard zips toward them on a two-wheeled electric vehicle.

"Run!" Sam shouts.

The three sleuths sprint across the parking lot.

From behind, the guard on the two-wheeled vehicle shouts after them, "Stop, you kids!"

"Keep going!" Sam shouts to her friends. "Once we're in the park, we can lose him!"

Cat isn't so sure, and running away from a security guard isn't like her.

But the gates are close. She thinks maybe Sam might be right.

"Uh-oh," Egg says out loud next to Cat.

"Please stop saying that!" Cat says, breathless.

But he's right. Up ahead, Sam skids to a stop. A moment later, Egg and Cat stop right behind her.

Standing in the middle of the open gate are Ms. Marco, Mr. Dawson, and Mr. Spade. Gum stands behind them, looking a little disappointed.

"Explain," Mr. Spade says, crossing his arms.

TURN THE PAGE.

The security guard comes to a stop beside them.

He turns to Mr. Dawson and says, "Saw them snooping around an old green station wagon on the north end," he says.

"Thanks, officer," Mr. Spade says. "I'll take it from here."

Mr. Spade leads the three detectives back into the parking lot.

"You too, James Shoo," he calls over his shoulder.

"Me?" Gum says. "I was just playing mini-golf."

"I don't know yet how you're involved," Mr. Spade says, "but I'm going to find out."

"Aw, man," Gum says. "I had to play extra mini-golf *and* I got in trouble anyway. No fair."

"Come on," Mr. Spade says. "You'll wait on the bus with Mel until the field trip is over. Don't worry," he continues. "I'm sure Mel has some back issues of *Bus Driver Monthly* he'd be happy to let you read."

THE END

TO FOLLOW ANOTHER PATH, TURN TO PAGE 11.

But from where Egg is hiding, he can't see inside Ana's locker. As quietly as he can, Egg slowly opens the door of the locker he's hiding in.

He steps out silently, but he still can't see inside her locker.

Knowing he has to get closer to see what's happening, he tiptoes toward her. Then he remembers the camera hanging around his neck — zoom lens!

He raises the camera to his eye as he walks. He zooms, closer and closer, until he can almost —

Bam!

Egg trips right over the wooden bench that runs along the center of the row. He tumbles to the floor, barely saving his camera from smashing to bits.

By the time he looks up, Ana has slammed her locker shut and is closing the padlock. She spins the combination wheel.

"You!" Ana says. "You're one of the kids who was bugging me when I was trying to study!"

"No!" Egg says. "I mean, we didn't mean to bug you!"

Ana spots his camera and says, "Are you taking pictures?!"

Sam suddenly tears around the corner, Cat and Gum close behind. "Come on!" Sam says, grabbing Egg's hand and pulling him along.

"Hey!" Ana shouts after them as they flee into the hallway. "Come back here!"

But they keep running, out of the building and across the plaza.

"We have to hide!" Sam says.

But it's too late, because right across the plaza are Mr. Dawson and Mr. Spade.

"Mr. Dawson!" Ana shouts from behind them as she exits the tan building. "Grab those kids!"

Mr. Spade and Mr. Dawson block the sleuths' path.

"What's going on here?" Mr. Spade asks.

TURN THE PAGE.

"I'll tell you what's going on," Ana says as she runs up to them and skids to a stop. "These four weirdo kids were taking photos of me by my locker!"

"That is *not* true," Cat says.

"And they interrogated me while I was trying to study!" Ana says.

"Well, that's true," Cat admits, "but — "

"What more do I need to say?" Ana asks. "They're harassing me."

Mr. Spade looks at his four students, his face going red. "I, for one, have heard enough," he says.

"But she stole the cards!" Sam says.

"Do you have proof?" Mr. Spade says.

"We were trying to get some proof!" Sam says.

"Not good enough, Samantha," Mr. Spade says. "Now you'll spend the rest of this field trip on the bus with Mel. March!"

THE END

To follow another path, turn to page 11.

"Well, my friends and I were in there for just a few moments," Cat goes on, "and the cat, Coal, managed to get hair on us."

"Oh, I see where you're going," Sam says.

"We'll get everyone to line up," Cat says, "and then check their clothes for coal-gray hairs."

Sam raises her eyebrows, impressed. "It might work," she says.

The sleuths, Mr. Spade, and Mr. Dawson go through the break room door. Mr. Dawson calls, "Listen up, everyone."

Cat steps forward. "Before we start, do any of you have a cat at home?"

The employees look at each other, confused. Then three slowly raise their hands.

"What color are your cats?" Cat asks.

"Mine's orange," says a woman on the end. "My dog is brown."

"I have two cats," says another. "Both are pitch black with a white spot on their faces."

Turn the page.

A tall man with a beard raises his hand. His name tag says Eugene.

"I have a Siamese," Eugene says. "She's tan."

"Great," Cat says. "Everyone please line up."

The staff look at Mr. Dawson. He nods.

When they are shoulder to shoulder, Cat examines each employee's shirt and slacks.

"What is this all about, Mr. Dawson?" asks a young woman toward the end of the line. She sounds nervous. "I have a lot of studying to do."

"Just another minute, Ana," Mr. Dawson says.

When Cat reaches Ana, the woman fidgets and picks at her clothes.

Cat glances at Sam. Sam winks and nods.

"Ana," Cat says, but before she can finish, Eugene bursts from the line and drops to his knees.

"Please, please!" he says. "Stop this inquisition. I confess!"

Cat's mouth drops open.

"*You* confess?" Sam says.

"Everyone is underpaid," Eugene says. "And I've had a bad cold," he says. "But I couldn't afford a sick day to rest. This was the best solution I could think of."

"Oh, you'll have plenty of time to rest now, Eugene," Mr. Dawson says. "You're fired."

Eugene slumps onto the floor.

"That was some good sleuthing, Cat!" Gum says.

"Thanks," Cat says. "But I thought it was Ana!"

Eugene looks up from the floor. "Really?" he says. "You mean I might have gotten away with it?"

Cat nods.

Eugene wails toward the ceiling like a baying hound.

"Yes, Ana's cleared and can go back to running the water-pistol game," Mr. Dawson says.

Sam's eyes go wide. "I just remembered," she says. "I still have to use the bathroom!"

THE END

To follow another path, turn to page 11.

"There's Dr. Lewis," Egg says as the four sleuths head back toward the mini-golf area.

This sixth-grade teacher is leaning on a lamppost just outside the eighteenth hole. Though her back is to them, they can tell from her bent head that she's looking at her phone.

As they get closer, they notice her thumbs rapid-fire tapping at the cell phone's screen.

"Dr. Lewis," Sam says, jogging up next to the teacher.

Dr. Lewis thrusts an index finger into the air to silence her, and then immediately goes back to texting.

"Okay," Sam mutters under her breath, shoving her hands into her pockets.

Her friends catch up and stand around her.

"And . . . done," Dr. Lewis says. She clicks off the phone's screen and slips it into the pocket of her white blazer.

She turns to Sam and smiles as if she's genuinely glad to be interrupted.

Sam struggles to return the smile. "We were wondering," Sam says, "did Mr. Spade seem . . . weird this morning at all?"

"You mean weirder than most days?" Dr. Lewis says, her eyebrows up. She laughs, but at the same time reaches into her pocket to pull out her phone again.

"I think she really likes that phone," Egg whispers to Cat.

"I'm kidding," Dr. Lewis goes on as she looks at her phone on and reads a text. "He seemed normal at breakfast, anyway."

"You had breakfast with him?" Sam asks.

Dr. Lewis hums, "Mm-hm."

"On the way down here?" Cat follows up.

"Mm-hm," Dr. Lewis says, distracted by the text she's typing. "At that little diner on Route 169."

Sam watches the teacher type for a while. "You get a lot of texts, huh?" Sam asks.

"Hmm?" Dr. Lewis says without looking up.

Turn to page 75.

"Well, well, well," Sam says as she strolls right up to Anton and his goons.

Of the four junior detectives, Sam is the only one who's never been intimidated by the three troublemakers.

"What do we have here?" Sam says, putting a hand on Anton's shoulder.

Gum, Egg, and Cat stand behind Sam.

Luca, Hans, and Anton hurry to hide what they're holding, but it's too late.

"Aha!" Gum says, pointing and smiling, his mouth wide open. "The cards! You have the stolen cards! I knew it!"

"He did know," Sam says, grinning. "He said so and everything."

Anton looks up at Luca and Hans. For a moment, it seems like he's going to give them the order to attack. But instead, he laughs.

TURN THE PAGE.

The goons exchange a look, and then they too begin to laugh — deep, throaty guffaws.

"I don't see what's so funny," Cat says, crossing her arms. "You three are in big trouble, and you've already ruined the morning for the rest of the sixth grade!"

"All right," Sam says. "What's the play, huh? You three are heading to the hoosegow, and here you are making with the yuk-yuks. What gives?"

Anton stops laughing. "What'd she say?" he asks Gum.

Gum shrugs.

Anton shakes his head. "Look, you dorks," he says. "These aren't the stolen cards. These are mine. I brought them from home."

"Then you won't mind showing Mr. Spade," Egg says. "And Mr. Dawson, the park manager."

"I didn't say that," Anton says. "You nerds mind your own business or Luca and Hans will make sure you do."

Sam glowers at him.

TURN TO PAGE 79.

"How far did those weasels go?" Sam asks.

She and her friends are deep into the park and there's still no sign of Anton and his goons.

They turn up the path and Gum grabs Sam's arm to stop her. "There they are," Gum says.

Egg raises his camera. "Never hurts to get some photos," he says.

Anton, Luca, and Hans are 50 yards ahead. Anton is down on his knees with one arm up inside a vending machine.

Sam, Gum, Egg, and Cat stroll up behind them.

"What do you nerds want?" Anton says. Luca and Hans turn and grunt at them.

"We were just wondering if you had anything to do with the missing cards," Sam says.

"Right," Anton says, getting up and dusting off his hands. "Because of course it was me. Even though the cards were already missing when we got here on the buses, same as you four weirdos."

TURN THE PAGE.

Sam opens her mouth to respond, but she can think of nothing to say.

"Now buzz off, dweeb patrol," Anton says.

The three troublemakers stroll off.

"We should follow them," Sam says. "Carefully."

Gum narrows one eye and nods.

Sam taps her nose.

"What are you two doing?" Egg says. "Come on."

The four sleuthing friends hurry to follow Anton.

Anton, Luca, and Hans reach a big tan building near the front plaza. They slip behind it.

"This might be our big break," Sam whispers. "Let's hurry."

The four friends find the boys standing behind the building. The sleuths hide off the path to watch.

"What are they doing?" Cat whispers.

"They're just standing there," Egg says as he takes photos. The back door of the building opens. "Whoa, look at that."

Turn to page 82.

"Nothing," Egg puts in. "So, you arrived here with Mr. Spade."

Dr. Lewis finishes her text and looks up at Egg, her eyebrows wrinkled in confusion. "Didn't I just say that?" she asks.

She slips her phone back into her pocket. "His car is such a mess!" she says, laughing. "I don't know how he could ever find folders or homework in that catastrophe on wheels."

"And did you get here way before the buses?" Sam asks. "I bet you two had a lot of time to waste, huh?"

"Oh, no," Dr. Lewis says as she pulls out her phone again. "I was barely out of the car when the buses pulled into the parking lot."

"Then Mr. Spade found out about the missing cards at the same time as everyone," Cat points out, "and definitely didn't get here early this morning to . . . to . . ."

Sam taps her nose.

TURN THE PAGE.

"Excuse me," Dr. Lewis says, this time putting her phone to her ear and stepping away. In a moment she's laughing and chatting on the phone.

"I prefer Mr. Spade," Gum says. "He isn't texting all the time."

"I'm not sure Mr. Spade has a cell phone," Egg says. "I once saw him using the old pay phone outside the school's main office."

"The point is," Sam says, "he has an alibi."

"Ooh, he should see a doctor about that," Gum says. "My grandma had an alibi once. Had to be in bed for two weeks."

"Um, an alibi means Mr. Spade can account for where he was and what he was doing when the crime was committed," Cat explains. "Shouldn't you know that after solving mysteries all the time?"

Gum shrugs and grins.

"In a way, it's good news," Egg points out. "I like Mr. Spade. I'm glad he didn't do it."

"That's true," Gum says, "but we didn't solve the crime, and I do *not* want to play any more mini-golf."

Just then, Mr. Spade strolls up to them with four clubs in one hand and a bucket of balls in the other. "Ah!" he says. "I'm so pleased to see you four back at the mini-golf course."

"Hi, Mr. Spade," Cat says, and even she has a hard time faking enthusiasm as he hands out the clubs among the sleuths.

"Join me for a round?" he says. "I think I finally have the hang of that tricky windmill on hole number seven!"

"Looks like mini-golf is exactly what we're doing the rest of the day!" Gum mumbles to Sam. The four friends follow Mr. Spade back to hole number one, shoulders slumped.

THE END

TO FOLLOW ANOTHER PATH, TURN TO PAGE 11.

"We'll tell Mr. Spade anyway!" Cat says, hiding behind Gum and Sam.

"Ha!" Anton says. "Go for it, Cat. Or is it *Dog*?"

Cat pouts at him.

Anton laughs and sneers at Sam. "Come on, boys," he says to Luca and Hans, and the three of them walk off, deeper into the park.

Gum, Sam, Cat, and Egg watch him go.

"I *am* going to 'go for it'!" Cat says, stamping one foot. "Come on. Let's find Mr. Spade."

The detectives find Mr. Spade at the mini-golf course and tell him everything.

Mr. Spade sighs. "I wish those three boys would stay out of trouble," he says. "I've been on the phone with Ms. Gutman . . . Oh, never mind. Where are they?"

"We saw them over by the — " Gum starts.

"That's fine," Mr. Spade says, looking past the kids. "Here they come now."

TURN THE PAGE.

Sure enough, Anton and his henchmen swagger up the path.

"You boys," Mr. Spade says. "Step up here."

"What's wrong, Mr. Spade?" Anton says in his most innocent-sounding voice.

It doesn't fool Mr. Spade for a minute. "Empty your pockets," he says.

Anton puts on a confused expression and turns out his pockets. His goons copy him. They've got phones, a couple of candies, and a business card for Anton's big sister, a computer specialist.

But none of them has the plastic cards.

"Hey, what's the big idea?" Sam says. "What'd you do with the cards?"

"Why, what cards, Samantha?" Anton asks.

"All right, all right," Mr. Spade says. "You three can go."

Anton, laughing, leads his goons away.

Mr. Spade puts his hands on his hips. "Come to think of it," he says to the detectives, "I got here before the buses, and the cards were already missing. Anton couldn't have done it."

"But we saw the cards!" Cat protests as Mr. Spade walks off.

Sam runs after Anton and grabs his shoulder to stop him. "Hey," she snaps. "Where are those cards?"

"What cards?" Anton says. "I have no idea what you're talking about." He laughs.

Sam narrows her eyes at Anton as her friends join her.

"And now you four had better watch your backs," Anton says. "Because Luca and Hans don't like tattletales."

The two henchmen growl.

"Not now," Anton says. "Let's go play some golf."

With that, the three troublemakers turn their backs on the sleuths and walk off.

"We," Gum says, "are in big trouble."

THE END

To follow another path, turn to page 11.

"Who's that guy?" Sam says.

He's a big guy in a black polo shirt and black pants. In one hand he holds a white cardboard box.

He steps right up to the three boys.

"He must be Hans's brother," Gum says. "They're like peas in a pod."

Sam nods. "An inside job," she says.

Gum taps his nose.

Sam narrows one eye and nods again.

Egg rolls his eyes. "Just listen," he says.

"Here you go," the big guy says, handing the box to Anton. His voice is deep and tough sounding. "This had better work."

"Don't worry, Gunther," Anton says. "My sister is a whiz at this. Give her one night, and every card in this box will be bursting with prize tickets."

"Whoa," Sam whispers. "It's a scam!"

"All of us will have as many ZCube game consoles as we want," Anton says.

"We'd better," Gunther says. "Or else."

Gunther retreats into the staff building.

"Come on," Anton says to the goons, and the three head back around the building.

The sleuths jump out from their hiding place. "Aha!" Sam says. "You are so busted!"

Anton stops. He takes out the cardboard box and throws it in the air. Then he takes off.

"Not so fast!" Sam says.

She springs after him, and Anton doesn't have a chance. In a moment, Sam has Anton by the collar in the middle of the plaza.

Before Anton's henchmen can pull Sam off, Mr. Spade and Mr. Dawson come running over.

"Samantha Archer, what are you doing?" Mr. Spade says.

"I think Anton can explain," Sam says, "with a little help from Gunther. Mr. Dawson can probably get ahold of him."

"Gunther?" Mr. Spade says. "You mean Hans's big brother?" He turns to Hans. "Hans, what does your brother have to do with this?"

TURN TO PAGE 85.

Hans stares at Mr. Spade.

"Does he work here?" Mr. Spade says.

Hans sniffs and grunts.

"I see," Mr. Spade says. He turns to Sam and asks again, "Does he work here?"

"He sure does," Sam says, and she goes on to explain the whole scam.

"This is more serious than I ever imagined," Mr. Dawson says. "I'll call the police — and all your parents," he adds, glaring at Anton and his henchmen.

"Well done, kids," Mr. Dawson says as he takes four plastic cards from his jacket pocket. "You've saved the park quite a lot of money. As a thank-you, these cards are truly loaded with prize tickets."

"Wow," Gum says. "So we could get the ZCubes Anton and his friends thought they would get."

Sam shakes her head. "It's like they always say," she adds. "Crime doesn't pay."

THE END

To follow another path, turn to page 11.

"It makes perfect sense," Sam says.

She walks fast across the park's central square, not noticing the kids milling around and talking.

"I don't know," Egg says. "Mr. Spade? A criminal?"

Cat hurries along next to Sam. "Criminal?" she says, her voice high. "But if he only took the cards so we'd all play mini-golf with him, that's not *really* a crime, is it?"

Something bright flashes and Cat is momentarily distracted by the kids in the square, but she turns back to Sam.

"I'm afraid it is, Cat," Sam says. She walks with her chin down and her eyes narrowed. "And if Mr. Spade committed this crime, he'll have to pay his debt to society."

"That's a little dramatic, isn't it?" Gum says.

But Sam shushes him. "There he is," Sam says, stopping and pointing at the seventh hole of the mini-golf course.

Mr. Spade stands poised over his golf ball, lining up a putt. His mustache flicks and twitches as he concentrates.

"Look at him," Sam says. "Pleased to have committed the perfect crime." She adds, "And now he's reaping the spoils."

Gum scratches his head. "He is?" he says. "Because it looks like he's playing mini-golf."

Sam nods. "But not for long," she says. "Come on."

With that, she leads her friends to the seventh hole.

"Mr. Spade," Sam says as she steps over the little wooden fence that acts as a border around the seventh-hole putting green. "Can we talk to you?"

"Shush!" Mr. Spade says. He doesn't take his eyes off the ball.

"But we — " Sam goes on.

"Shh!" Mr. Spade repeats. He says in a whisper, "This hole has been giving me trouble all morning. I'll help you in a moment."

TURN THE PAGE.

The teacher twists his face in concentration as he gingerly taps the ball with his club, sending it rolling toward the windmill obstacle.

"I think I've got it this time," he says — just before the ball bounces off one of the windmill's blades and flies off the course.

Mr. Spade and the four sleuths watch as the ball bounces along the park's blacktop paths, rolls down a hill, and finally bounces into a fountain with a plop.

Mr. Spade's face goes red. "That," he says, clenching his teeth, "is — the fifth — ball — today."

"Oh," Cat says, taking Sam's elbow. "Um, we'll talk to you later, Mr. Spade. Sorry to bother you."

Sam shakes off Cat's arm. She says, "Mr. Spade, I've known you a long time. You've been my teacher for almost a year. We respect each other."

"What?" Mr. Spade says, looking at Sam, confused.

TURN TO PAGE 96.

"They'll probably be over by the mini-golf course," Gum says as he and his friends jog across the park. "It's not far from the office."

Sam nods and picks up speed. If they don't get to Mr. Dawson and Mr. Spade quickly, who knows what those three troublemakers Anton, Luca, and Hans will do with the stolen cards in the meantime.

Leaving her friends behind, Sam kicks it into high gear. She spots Mr. Spade — tall and lanky, with a head of messy brown hair and a thick beard that could have been spotted from a mile away — at the eighteenth hole.

"Mr. Spade!" she calls, at just the wrong moment.

He flinches, knocking what should have been an easy putt right off the green and into a pond.

"Oh, sorry, Mr. Spade," Sam says. "Didn't mean to mess up your shot. You shouldn't count that one on your scorecard."

TURN THE PAGE.

"Hmm, you're probably right," Mr. Spade says. "I was interfered with. I'll just get another ball from Mr. Dawson." He smiles at the sleuth.

"Right," Sam says, grabbing Mr. Spade's wrist as he turns away. "Speaking of Mr. Dawson, I need to speak to you *and* him. We just saw Anton, Luca, and Hans with the stolen cards!" Sam finishes.

Mr. Spade's smile drops away. "I'll get Mr. Dawson," he says. "Can you take us to where you saw them?"

Sam nods. "Yup," she says. "but hurry."

In a few moments, Mr. Dawson joins the group and he, Mr. Spade, and Sam find the other three sleuths not far along the path.

"Oh, man," Gum says, rubbing his hands together. "We're finally gonna bust Anton."

Mr. Spade shoots him a disapproving look.

"I mean," Gum says, "we fight crime for justice!"

Together, the group walks quickly across the amusement park.

They spot Anton and his goons on the midway.

When the three troublemakers see the group coming toward them, they quickly veer away.

"Just a minute," Mr. Spade calls out in his you're-in-trouble voice. "Come over here, please."

"He says 'please,'" Sam whispers to Cat, "but he ain't askin'."

Cat giggles and covers her mouth.

The three crooks walk toward them.

"What seems to be the problem, Mr. Spade?" Anton asks.

"I need you boys to empty your pockets," Mr. Spade says.

"What?" he says. "Why?"

"Like you don't know!" Gum says.

"We saw you with the cards!" Cat says.

Anton sneers at her. Luca and Hans snarl.

But the three boys empty their pockets onto a picnic table, and sure enough, Anton has a thick stack of plastic cards, a magnetic strip on the back of each one.

TURN TO PAGE 99.

Gum, Egg, Cat, and Sam head into the plaza to find chaperones.

Since the park is closed for everyone except the field trip from Franklin Middle School, it's not hard to find them. They're the only adults in the park who aren't teachers and aren't wearing park staff uniforms.

After about ten minutes, they've spoken to most of the adults. They all said the same thing: "The blue-haired girl seems kind of . . . odd."

Chloe Marshfield.

"They just think she's odd because she's . . . well, odd," Cat points out. "That doesn't mean she committed a crime."

"We don't have any other leads," Gum says as he spots Chloe sitting on the bench. "She's right where we left her. Might as well talk to her — it's better than mini-golfing."

The four friends walk over to her.

"You again," Chloe says without looking up from her sketch.

"You're so talented," Cat says.

"Thanks," Chloe says, smiling.

"Listen," Sam says. "We gotta ask you: Did you steal the missing cards?"

"In response to that question," Chloe says, "let me ask you a question."

"Um, okay," Sam says.

"When did the buses get here?" Chloe says.

Before the detectives can answer, Chloe goes on, "And when did the cards get stolen?"

She goes on again before the friends can speak, "So could I have done it? Is it even possible?"

The four friends look at each other.

"I guess you're right," Egg says. "The cards were missing before the buses got here, so that means anyone who was on the buses couldn't have done it."

"Sorry, Chloe," Cat says.

"No problem," Chloe says. "Bye."

The four friends head back to the front plaza and spot one more adult they haven't spoken to yet.

TURN TO PAGE 95.

"Excuse us," Cat says as they walk up to the woman standing near the the ticket booth and the fence.

She's tall and pale, with a lopsided haircut. Unlike the other adults, she's not looking at her phone. She just stares into the distance.

"Hmm?" she says, not taking her eyes off the horizon.

"Did you see anything suspicious during the field trip?" Cat asks. "We're investigating those missing cards, and — "

"Nope," the woman says. She takes a little pad and pencil — kind of like the ones Sam carries — and writes something down.

"What's she doing?" Gum whispers to Sam.

Sam shrugs. "Maybe she's a detective too," she says.

"Nothing weird happened here all day. Besides the weirdness of life, of course," the woman says. She scratches some more writing into her notebook. "And I'm not a detective. I'm a poet."

TURN TO PAGE 103.

"I'll be blunt," Sam goes on, not listening. She puts her fists on her hips.

"Mr. Spade," Sam continues, "did you steal the park's missing cards so we'd have no choice but to play mini-golf — for free — all day?"

Mr. Spade's eyes go wide. He stares at Sam in disbelief for what seems to Cat, Egg, and Gum to be an eternity.

"Of all the . . . ," he says, flustered, his face growing redder by the second. "I can't — I don't — "

"He's not denying it," Gum whispers loudly to Sam.

Mr. Spade glares at Gum. Gum smiles at Mr. Spade.

"Wait here a moment," Mr. Spade says, eerily calm.

He shoulders his club, steps off the course, and walks purposefully toward the office.

Cat glances at Egg. Egg shrugs.

When Mr. Spade returns, he has Mr. Dawson with him. "Mr. Dawson, would you kindly explain to these fine *detectives* what happened this morning?"

Mr. Dawson throws him a strange look, but he shrugs and then breaks into a grin. "We have cards! One of my employees found out the entire batch we had was defective. So she called the distributor last night and asked for an emergency stash for today. Coal — that's our office cat — knocked her note behind a file cabinet. Silly kitty." Mr. Dawson smiles fondly. Sam sneezes.

"Geez, Sam, are you allergic to the *idea* of cats?" Gum asks.

Sam ignores him. She sticks her chin out. "Well, Mr. Spade, did you ruin that batch of cards on purpose? Did you come here last night, break into the office, then . . . then . . ." She trails off, knowing she sounds ridiculous.

Mr. Spade shakes his head. "I'm disappointed in you, Samantha. Not only did you not have any proof, but you also didn't trust me. Evidently you *don't* have respect for me."

TURN THE PAGE.

Cat, with tears in her eyes, says, "We're so sorry, Mr. Spade."

Egg chimes in, "Yeah, we really do respect you."

A cheer goes up through the park and Sam sees the Ferris wheel start turning.

Gum swallows. "Okay! Funny mistake, eh, Mr. Spade? We'll just take our cards now and go." He clears his throat and laughs awkwardly.

Mr. Spade looks down his glasses at him. "I don't think so, James. I think maybe some time thinking about falsely accusing your teachers might be the best course of action for you four."

Gum and Sam groan. Egg looks down. Cat nods.

Mr. Dawson pipes up. "They can help our chef in the cafeteria! Her name is Kelly. She likes experimenting." He wrinkles his nose. "Sometimes it doesn't work. I'll be honest," he says, "they do call her Smelly Kelly around here."

Mr. Spade smiles. "That sounds perfect."

THE END

TO FOLLOW ANOTHER PATH, TURN TO PAGE 11.

"See?" Sam says, crossing her arms and grinning. "The stolen cards, right there."

Mr. Dawson picks up a few of the cards and looks closely at them. "Well, this is odd," he says.

"What's that?" Mr. Spade says.

"These are not the stolen cards at all!" Mr. Dawson says.

"What?!" say Gum, Sam, Cat, and Egg all at once.

Anton smiles. "See that?" he says. "I didn't do anything. Now I think the dork-tectives here owe me an apology."

Mr. Dawson continues, "I'm afraid this is much worse, in fact. This is a counterfeit gaming card."

Mr. Spade's eyebrows go up.

Sam's jaw drops open.

"That's ridiculous," Anton says.

Mr. Dawson turns to Mr. Spade. "I can't be sure until I bring this to the office and run them through the machine," he says, "but I'd bet these are phony cards with phony winning tickets on them."

TURN THE PAGE.

"You've seen this before?" Mr. Spade asks.

Mr. Dawson nods. "It was a few weeks before we caught on," he admits. "It wasn't until we'd given out some very expensive prizes to some very dishonest visitors that we discovered the trick."

Mr. Spade turns to Anton and glares at him.

"What?" Anton says. "They're not counterfeit or whatever. He's wrong!"

"Then we'll just bring these back to Mr. Dawson's office," Mr. Spade says, "and check them on the computer."

He and Mr. Dawson turn around to head back to the office.

"Wait!" Anton says. He looks at his feet. "He's right. They're fake."

"Anton Gutman!" Cat says. "How could you?"

"I didn't know it would be a big deal!" he says. "My sister made them for me. She said she read something online about how some kids all got free ZCube systems by turning in fake cards."

"There's no such thing as a free lunch, Gutman," Sam says, looking down her nose at him.

He squints at her. "Weirdo."

"You boys, come to the office. I'll have to call your parents. And your sister," Mr. Dawson says.

With that, Mr. Dawson escorts Anton and his goons back toward the office.

"Good job, investigators," Mr. Spade says to the four friends, before he, too, heads back toward the front of the park.

Sam sighs. "Well, we finally busted Anton."

"Yeah," Gum says, crossing his arms. "Just for the wrong crime."

The four walk glumly toward the front of the park.

"One more round of mini-golf?" Cat says.

Gum throws his head back and groans. "Worst. Trip. Ever."

THE END

TO FOLLOW ANOTHER PATH, TURN TO PAGE 11.

"Oh," Sam says, feeling her face get hot. "Sorry."

"Don't be sorry," she says. "Anyway, I can't help you. I've been here since before the buses got here, and I haven't seen anything weird."

"Wait," Gum says. "Before the buses?"

The woman nods. "I decided to take the car," she says. "My daughter and I arrived fifteen minutes early or so."

"Your daughter?" Sam says. "Don't tell me."

The woman finally looks away from the horizon and smiles at Sam. "You probably know her," the woman says. "Chloe Marshfield. I'm Kate Marshfield."

"Then she didn't come on the bus!" Sam says. "Thanks, Chloe's mom. We gotta go."

The four friends hurry back to Chloe's sketching bench.

"I take it you met Kate?" Chloe says. "She didn't recite to you, did she?"

"No," Sam says, "but she did tell us — "

TURN THE PAGE.

"That I wasn't on the bus," Chloe says. "Listen, I never said I was on the bus. I never even said I didn't take the cards, did I?"

"Not exactly, no," Egg says.

"Okay then," Chloe says as she sets her sketchbook down on the bench beside her. She opens the flap of her bag and pulls out a slim, white cardboard box.

"Here are the cards," she says. "You solved the case again!"

"I don't get it," Cat says as Sam takes the box. "Why'd you do it?"

Chloe picks up her sketchbook and shrugs. "We were early, and I had nothing to do," she says. "I figured it would make the trip fun for *you* guys."

"That's a little . . . ," Sam says, "weird."

"Kind of endearing, though," Cat says.

"Besides," Chloe goes on, "with the rides all stopped, I was able to sketch the Ferris wheel."

With that, she closes her sketchbook and stands. "I hope you guys aren't mad," she says. "And I hope you had a fun morning. I'll go return the cards to Mr. Dawson if you want."

Sam gives her a crooked glare.

Chloe shrugs. "Or you guys can," she says. "What's the expression? 'Your collar'?"

"Right," Sam says. "But we won't tell anyone it was you."

"We'll just say we found them," Gum says.

"What?" Cat says. "We can't — "

Sam elbows her gently.

"Um, okay," Cat says. "We found them."

Chloe picks up her bag. "Thanks," she says. "See ya." She strolls off toward the front plaza.

The four friends walk together toward the office.

Sam stares after Chloe. "She's weirder than we are," Sam says. "Right?"

Gum pats her on the back. "Eccentric," he says. He grabs the box from her. "We're eccentric."

THE END

TO FOLLOW ANOTHER PATH, TURN TO PAGE 11.

literary news

MYSTERIOUS WRITER REVEALED!

Steve Brezenoff is the author of the Field Trip Mysteries, the Museum Mysteries, and the Ravens Pass series of thrillers, as well as three novels for older readers. Steve lives in Minneapolis, Minnesota, with his wife, Beth, and their two children, Sam and Etta.

arts & entertainment

ARTIST IS KEY TO SOLVING MYSTERY, SAY POLICE

Marcos Calo lives happily in A Coruña, Spain, with his wife, Patricia (who is also an illustrator), and their daughter, Claudia. When Marcos and Patricia aren't drawing, they like to go on long walks by the sea. They also watch a lot of films and eat Nutella sandwiches. Yum!

A Detective's Dictionary

eccentric – odd or strange, but in an endearing way

flank - to be positioned on both sides or one side of a person or thing

glowering – a facial expression that shows anger

hoosegow – another name for prison

miming – to make gestures with your hands to show something, while not talking

par – at the level of something else; in golf, "on par" means the number of hits suggested by a golf course that a golfer should try to stay under

strike - to band together with fellow employees and refuse to work until conditions in the workplace are better

yuk-yuks – laughs

FURTHER INVESTIGATIONS

CASE #YCSFTMTCCSI7

1. Sam says at one point that "crime doesn't pay." What do you think that expression means?

2. A few times the sleuths accuse people without evidence. How much evidence is enough to show that someone is guilty?

3. Chloe Marshfield seems to be doing the sleuths a favor with the cards. Do you think she is? Would you have told an adult what she'd done?

IN YOUR OWN DETECTIVE'S NOTEBOOK . . .

1. Eugene wanted to organize the workers for a strike. Write a letter from him to the employees trying to convince them to join his movement for more pay.

2. The four friends accuse Mr. Spade of committing a crime. Write a letter of apology from all four of them to Mr. Spade. Make sure that each character says something to him.

3. Kate Marshfield is a poet. What kind of a poem is she writing? Pretend you are her and write a poem about the amusement park.

Ready to choose your next MYSTERY?

Check out all the books in the You Choose Stories Field Trip Mysteries!

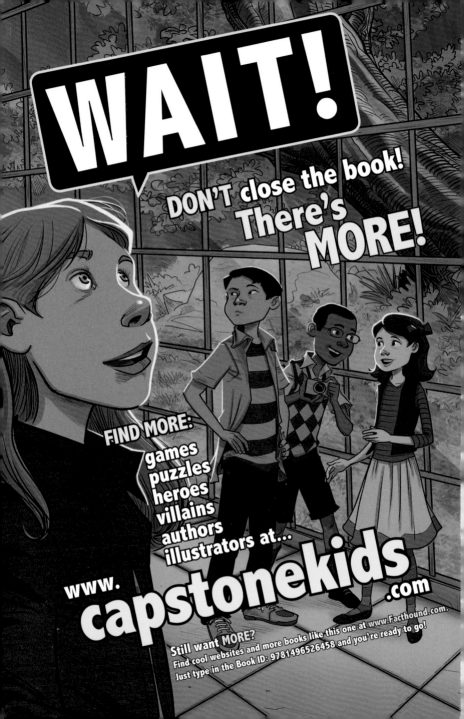